Fun Dog, Sun Dog

story by
Deborah Heiligman

illustrations by
Tim Bowers

SCHOLASTIC INC.
New York Toronto London Auckland Sydney
Mexico City New Delhi Hong Kong Buenos Aires

ISBN-13: 978-0-439-89196-7
ISBN-10: 0-439-89196-5

Text copyright © 2005 by Deborah Heiligman. Illustrations copyright © 2005 by Tim Bowers.
All rights reserved. Published by Scholastic Inc., 557 Broadway, New York, NY 10012,
by arrangement with Marshall Cavendish. SCHOLASTIC and associated logos are
trademarks and/or registered trademarks of Scholastic Inc.

12 11 10 9 8 7 6 5 4 3 2 1   7 8 9 10 11/0

Printed in the U.S.A.   08

This edition first printing, January 2007

The text of this book is set in Coop Flaired.

The illustrations are rendered in acrylic paint on gessoed three-ply bristol board.

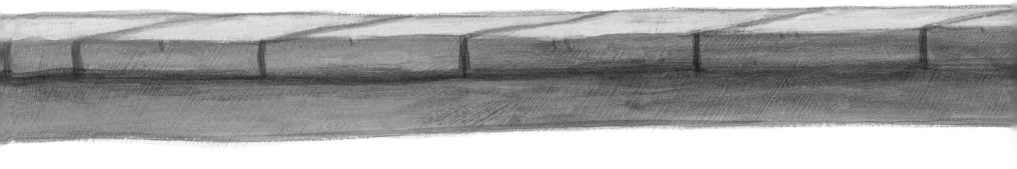

For Tinka, and for her friends Honeybee, Marigold, and Trippy –D.H.

To my friend, Jeff –T.B.

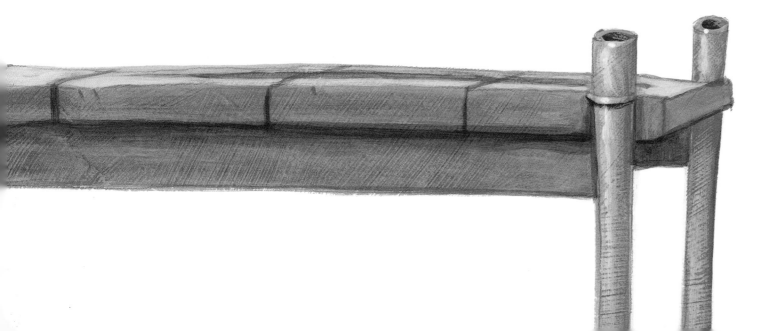

Tinka is a sweet dog,
a treat dog,
a jumping-up-to-greet dog.

A fun dog,
a sun dog,
a run-and-run-and-run dog.

A ride dog,
a slide dog,
a stay-right-by-my-side dog.

A beach dog,
a reach dog,
a something-new-to-teach dog.

Tinka is a dandy dog,
a sandy dog,
a snatching-all-my-candy dog.

A howl dog,
a yowl dog,
a crawl-beneath-my-towel dog.

An ocean dog,
a motion dog,
a grabbing-suntan-lotion dog.

A sticky dog,
an icky dog,
an icky-sticky-licky dog.

Tinka is a hot dog,
a trot dog,
a runs-away-a-lot dog.

A fair dog,
a bear dog,
an I-don't-want-to-share dog.

A busy dog,
a dizzy dog,
a soda-is-too-fizzy dog.

Tinka is a park dog,
a bark dog,
a take-me-home-it's-dark dog.

A night dog,
a fright dog,
a something's-not-quite-right dog.

A *Hey!* dog,
a sprayed dog,
a skunk-got-in-the-way dog.

Tinka is a stink dog,
a blink dog,
a too-big-for-the-sink dog.

A tub dog,
a rub dog,
a scrub-a-dub-a-dub dog.

Tinka is a prancy dog,
a dancy dog,
a brushed-and-combed-and-fancy dog.

A nap dog,
a wrap dog,
a climb-up-in-my-lap dog.

A care dog,
a share dog,
a when-I-need-her-there dog.